For
Sira
Stampe
& Sigge

Thanks to
Sasha Middleton
for the nits

First published in hardback in Great Britain by HarperCollins Children's Books in 2014

First published in paperback in 2015   10 9 8 7 6 5 4 3 2 1

ISBN 978-0-00-746304-6   HarperCollins Children's Books is a division of HarperCollins Publishers Ltd.

Text and illustrations copyright © David Mackintosh 2014
Designed and lettered by David Mackintosh   **www.davidmackintosh.co.uk**

Visit our website at: **www.harpercollins.co.uk**
Printed and bound in China.

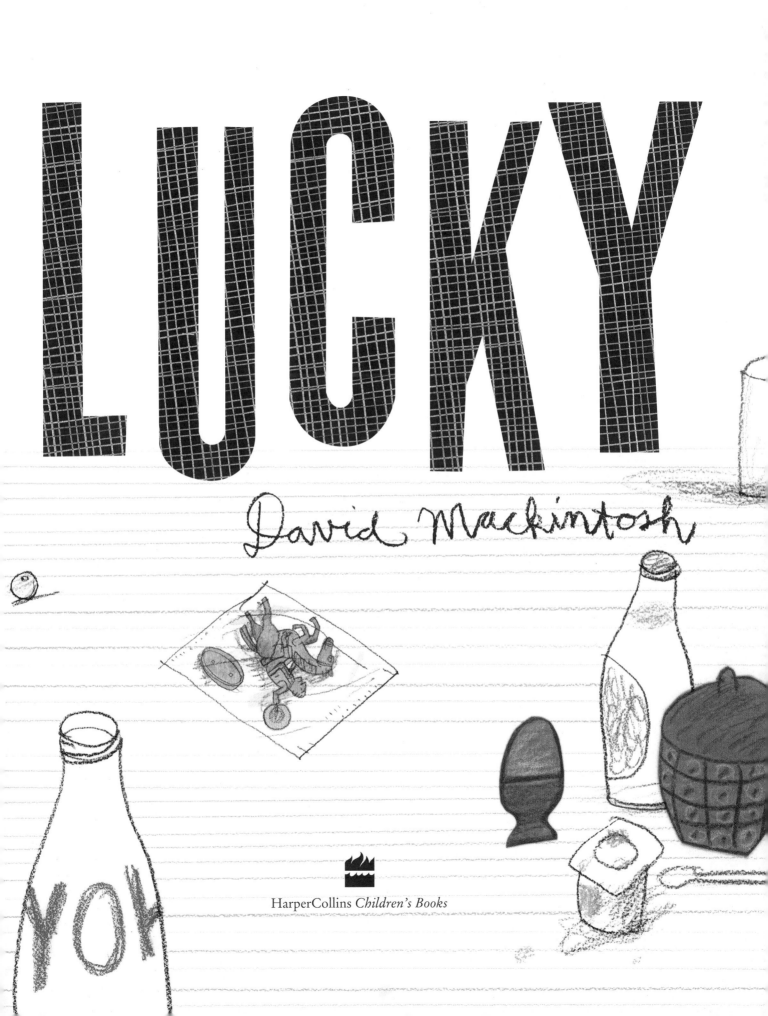

LUCKY

David Mackintosh

HarperCollins *Children's Books*

We're having a surprise at dinner tonight. Mum says so.

"WHAT IS IT?!"
my brother says.

"Just wait and see,"
says Mum.

My brother Leo
thinks it's crinkly
chips.

But
I start
thinking...

Last time we had a surprise,
I got a new bike.
Well... it won't be a new bike.

"*Yeah*, it's not your birthday," says Leo.

It must be even better than that.

Hey! Maybe it's tickets to
The Amazing Yo-Yo Super Show
at the town hall.

"Dad *said* we could go!"
my brother shouts.

But the Super Show finished last week. *Phooey.*

Maybe it's a brand new car! My brother thinks our old one smells funny.

Hmmm.
Dad likes our car.
He always washes it.

I have an idea...

MAYBE WE'RE GETTING A SWIMMING POOL IN the backyard.

"We'll need chlorine and ear plugs *too*," Leo says.

But we live in a high apartment and don't have a back-yard.

So that can't be it.

Hey... we might be getting a lift!

But Mum says that climbing stairs is good for our calves.

Just maybe... my very own room,

so I won't have to share with Leo for one second more.

But I doubt it. It took Dad ages to even put the cat flap in for our dog Abraham.

I GIVE UP.

I try
and
think of
something
that
will
take
my
mind
off
guessing
what
the
surprise
will
be.

Then,

I start
to think
that
there
won't
be a
surprise
at all.

Sometimes
grown-ups say
things they don't
really mean.

This could be
one of those times.

Today, we have our visit with Doctor Karen.

That's when Leo says,

"HEY!
I bet we're going to Hawaii for two weeks: all expenses paid!"

Leo says,

In Hawaii you drive about in golf carts and have spending money and drinks with fruit in them.

And... *There are erupting volcanoes there, with rivers of boiling lava and clouds of rotten egg gas.*

Plus... *To protect against volcanoes and falling coconuts, people wear grass skirts, flower necklaces and strum tiny guitars called ukuleles.*

But Hawaii looks expensive... we usually stay at home watching TV and arguing on holidays.

WELCOME BACK... and now the moment you've been waiting for when one LUCKY LISTENER has the CHANCE to WIN one of two AMAZING DREAM HOLIDAYS to a TROPICAL PARADISE destination of their CHOICE

So...

MUM AND DAD MUST HAVE WON THE HOLIDAY IN A COMPETITION!

Maybe Leo IS right: we ARE going to Hawaii for two weeks!

**On the outing,
I tell Lance Campbell.**

Who tells
Melody Diaz,

who tells
Penny Kurtz,

who tells
Sheldon Robe,

who tells
Hani Sherbet,

who tells
Bernard Joy,

who tells
Honey Garrett,

who tells
Felicity Singh,

**that my family
has won a
competition
to fly to Hawaii
for two weeks.**

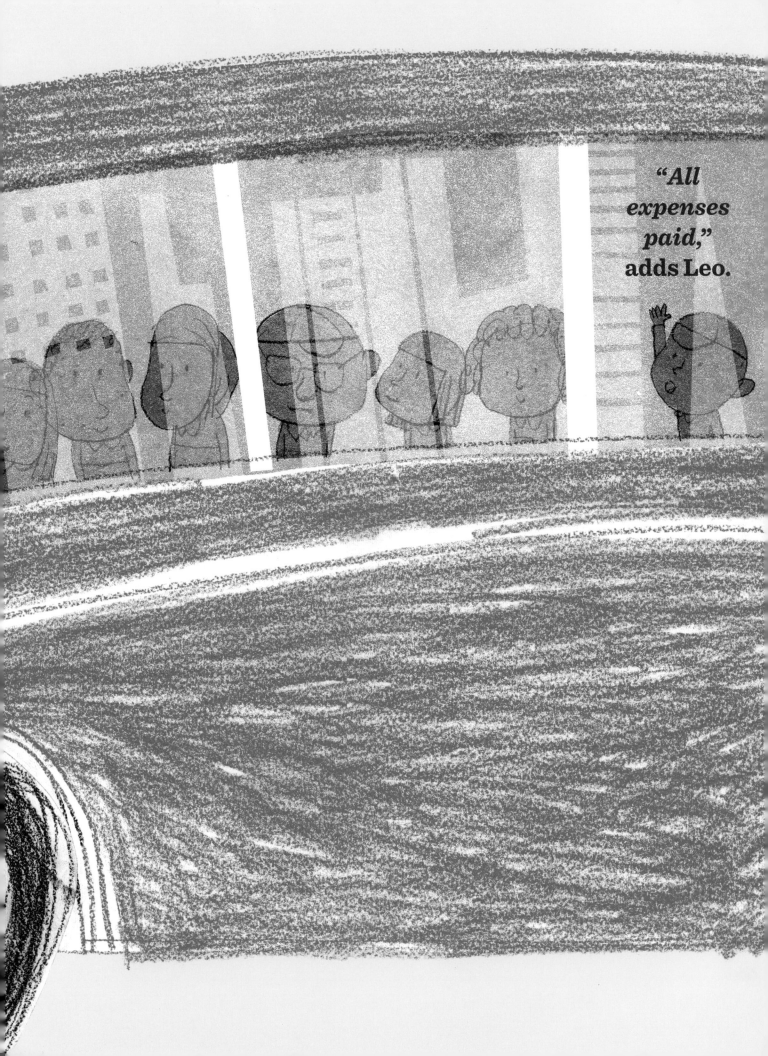

"*All expenses paid*," adds Leo.

I tell Miss Stamp that I won't be at school for two weeks because I'm flying to Hawaii on holiday. And I'm asked to talk about Hawaii to the class.

Afterwards, the Head Teacher says that this is the first time in history that anyone from our school has ever won a holiday.

To celebrate,
we're all allowed
ten minutes free time.

After school, me and my brother rush home, faster than ever.

"Let's get a milkshake from Giorgio's!" Leo yells.

No. No time for milkshakes.

"Are you going to watch *Jumpy Jim?*" he puffs.

No time for TV. We need plenty of time to pack our things for Hawaii, and we'll be catching a plane.

Dad once told me
You can't be late for planes.

**When we get there,
I tell mum that SHE'LL be
surprised because Leo and
me have already guessed
how lucky...**

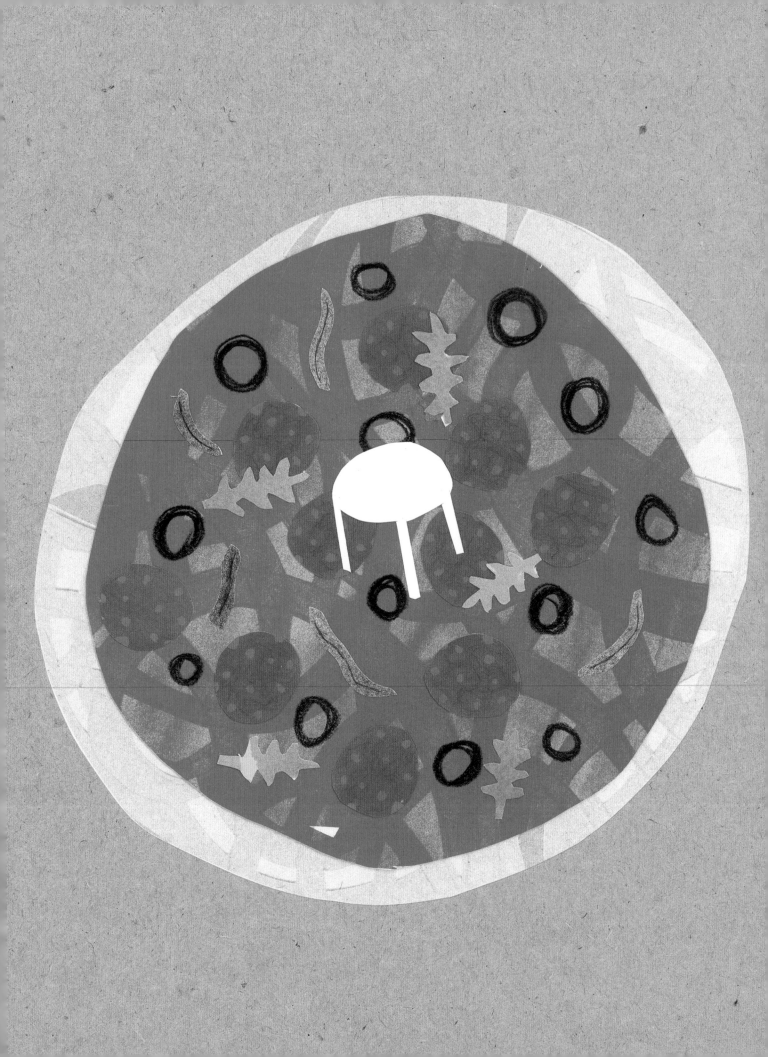

"PIZZA!" shouts Mum.

"WOO-HOO!" shouts Leo.

Pizza? *Pizza?*
I ask if she's sure
the surprise isn't
meant to be two
weeks in Hawaii,
because she won
a competition on
the radio.

Hawaii? *Hawaii?*
Mum laughs and
slices the pizza
with a little
wheel.

I don't feel very hungry
so I go to my room for a while.

I can hear Leo blabbing about
what happened at school
today. Especially the part
about Hawaii and how we all
got free time outside.

Mum is laughing, and Dad
makes a loud snorting noise
like a horse. Then *he* begins
laughing, and I can hear him
playing Leo's stupid guitar.

*What will I tell Miss Stamp
tomorrow?*

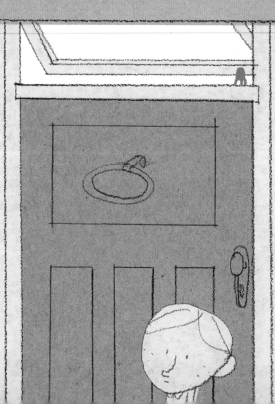

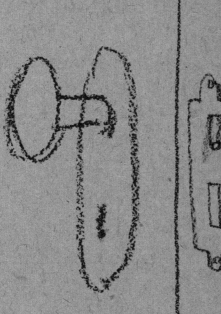

Soon,
Leo is at
the door.
But I'm
still not
hungry.

"Come on – it's a *different* surprise."

"It's Hawaiian Pizza!"

shouts Leo.

Then he calls our banana
splits Hawaiian Ice Cream.

Sometimes, Leo makes
my whole family laugh.
Including me. And I don't
even *like* pineapple.

He's good like that.

But I still don't want to share a room with him.